Apollo –
a dachshund tells his story

1st English Edition 2024

Anne Teutschbein-Licha

© 2024 Anne Teutschbein-Licha
Manufactoring and Publishing: BoD - Books on Demand, Norderstedt
ISBN: 978-3-7597053-9-6

The book is dedicated to my parents and my brother,
they made it possible for me to let a little dachshund into
my heart as a child and they stoically endured every failed puddle,
– and my husband, who can't be bothered by 7 dachshunds
has been deterred and has been infected.

Apollo says thank you very much to mistress's colleagues, who
always stepped in when the dachshund was in need,
so that mistress could be with us.
Thanks also to all veterinarians of the clinic in Hofheim, who have
always helped and were and always are there for us when things
got tricky, became serious and difficult.

Special thanks to Mrs. Regina Mitchell for the loving translation
and proofreading of my book.

Foreword

A little dachshund man very big, Apollo – a dachshund tells his and his family's story. Many small experiences make a big whole. Apollo would like to share his adventures and many experiences with you, and all dachshund enthusiasts and those who might want to become one. This book is intended to take you into a small world, which sometimes lies hidden, with all its beautiful and sometimes sad times.

Have fun reading and dreaming.
Your Apollo

Name translations:

aus der Götterdämmerung	from the twilight of the goddes
Luna	moon goddes
Flo	floo
Ceres / Chloe	goddes demeter / goddes of fertility
Zofe von der schönen Weide	maid from the beautiful pasture
Ares	god of war
Apollo	god of the light / art / music
Bendis	greek hunting goddes
Bacchus	god of the wine

pollo –

a dachshund tells his story

It was on a cold January night – Oh, I haven't even introduced myself yet, I'm Apollo aus der Götterdämmerung, a short-haired miniature dachshund, a little heartbreaker with a long nose, floppy ears and a look that can soften stones – when my brother and I came into the world.

Zofe
with Apollo and Ares
(1 week old)

My brother's name is Ares aus der Götterdämmerung, my mom is Zofe von der schönen Weide and my dad is the proud Alf von der Teckeltatze. So, now you know my family, well actually not quite yet. There are two two-legged friends, where my mom and we two brothers live. The rest of our rascals I will introduce to you later.

Now first of all about us. As I said, we were born on a cold January night. Outside, the cold north wind blew its song. We were born blind and deaf. So in the begin-

Zofe
with Apollo and Ares
(2 days old)

Zofe
with Apollo and Ares
(14 days old)

ning we didn't notice much of our surroundings. Only the warmth of our mom when she cleaned and suckled us. She always snuggled up very close to us.

Delightful! Her tongue tickled nicely when she cleaned us and when she cleaned us after dinner, she was very, very thorough. Sometimes we whined because we didn't want that. She would massage our tummies so we could do our big and little business. She would then clean everything up. She was always very clean.

*Apollo
with Mom and Brother
(3 weeks old)*

When we were 10 days old, we opened our eyes. What all was there to see. We explored our whelping box, crawled around in it and looked for the exit. Mom had a lot to do. My brother and I now also got to know our two-legged friends. Every few hours she came to play with us. But first we were weighed, examined and turned upside down. When we were 2 weeks old we became medicine. My two-legged friend said, we have to eat it often now. It was a worm cure and we should get used to it. It did not taste good at all. My brother and I trampled and kicked, but it was no use. She was even more thorough than our mommy.

Apollo
(7 weeks old)

Apollo
and his Plush Pig
(5 weeks old)

We are now 4 weeks old and have continued to explore our surroundings. The ground under our feet is always nice and warm, and we like to lie all stretched out and bask. The world is beautiful. Mom's milk bar is open around the clock, we play and romp, climb around on our two-legged friends and with our little pointed teeth we nibble on everything. Much to the chagrin of our two-legged friend. Mom said that the two-legged friends are our mistress and master. Funny names, but good. She always brings food for mom and for us. Mom's milk, however, tastes much better and mistress is quite desperate because we don't want to eat anything else.

Today was a particularly exciting day. We were allowed to go out into the big wide world. It was great there. So many new smells, sounds and other dachshunds. Mom was very nervous. The others were Aunt Luna, Aunt Flo and a roughhaired dachshund named Rumpel. He was huge and very scary. His fur was not as soft as ours and it was sticking out everywhere. He grumbled at us. That didn't matter at all, we tried to pluck him by his beard and tail.

When it became too much for him, he left. We were allowed into the garden and went exploring. Soon we were

hungry and begged our mom. Quickly cuddle up to her, eat and then into the land of dreams.

That was a nice time. We made discovery tours through the apartment of our two-legged friends. There were many other animals there. Such funny little ones, they ran through their cages and squealed. Mom always stood in front of them and wanted to catch them. In another cage it twittered, like in the garden. The feathers landed on our noses and bobbed up and down. In the evening, when we were all tired, we were allowed to join our mistress on an object she called a sofa. Snuggled up in warm blankets, lying on our backs with our feet in the air, we enjoyed life.

One fine day, I just stretched my dachshund snout in the garden, I saw something black little crawling along the door. My curiosity was aroused ... let's, go there. All of a sudden it nipped at my little mouth, Helpeeeee I thought, the bug wants to eat me. I ran squealing and whining through the garden and then back into the house. My mistress and everyone came running to save me. Finally my mistress had me in her arms and ... started laughing. Outrageous, I am being eaten and my mistress is laughing. Very quickly she picked the bug off my chaps and put it in the grass. She said: „Apollo, that is only a grain beetle". So what, I thought to myself, such a huge beast on me little dachshund man, who knows what can happen there. After everything had calmed down, I first snuggled up to my mom and was comforted, she didn't laugh at me, she cleaned me and I was allowed to suck her little ear to fall sleep.

When we were eight weeks old, our mistress said we must be vaccinated so that we do not get sick. We got a shot, that itched, maybe like many small ants. Our mistress said we shouldn't make such a fuss, it would stop in a minute.

One day two bipeds came to us. They cuddled us and said how cute we were. Then mistress took us in her arms and suddenly it pinched and pricked my ear. I thought, another vaccination. But no, we got tattooed. I was so scared that I forgot how brave I was and had to whine. My brother was much braver than me. He is also much bigger and much calmer. He looks at everything from a

Zofe
with Apollo and Ares
(7 weeks old)

distance. Then he decides what to do. I am a little sca-redy-cat, my mistress says. I see it differently, I am just cautious! My ear was burning a little bit and itching. I quickly ran to my mom and got me comfort. When the two-legged friends were gone, peace returned.

We are now already getting real food. Delicious venison, low-fat quark and dry food. But nothing comes close to mom's milk. Unfortunately, she doesn't want us to suckle her anymore. Our little teeth hurt her.

But even the most beautiful time is over once. Today was a sad day. My brother Ares has left us. My mistress was very sad. She says Ares is now called Bony and gets a new family. But we are his family. Mom was also very sad. She searched and searched for him. I comforted her and cuddled with her. Will we ever see him again?

The days go by and I am half a year old. In the meantime I am house-trained. That means I am already big and do my business outside, like mom and the others. My teeth change and I lose my pointed little teeth. They are ex-changed for my permanent teeth. Now it doesn't hurt the others so much when we play. I even fought for my place with my mistress. In the evening, when everyone goes to sleep, I should sleep in my basket. I did not see that at all, so completely alone. Whining, whining, whining and putting on the saddest look, I was allowed to go to bed with her. That was a hard piece of work, I can tell you. My mistress wanted to stay tough, but nobody can resist me. I have kept my place at the foot of the bed until today.

I can also run really fast. My master was playing with a rustling thing, so I went for it, bit and pulled. One rattle,

Apollo (l.) and Ares (r.)
(1 year old)

one tear and I was the proud winner. It wagged behind me. Master screamed and scolded. I did not know why at all. My mistress explained to me that I had broken my master's book. He reads stories in it. I was so sorry. So I went to him and whined until I was allowed on his lap, then I licked his face. He laughed and was no longer angry.

Sometimes I think about my brother, I wonder how he is doing. Mistress often talks to his new family and says that he is doing well. Soon we will go on vacation and visit him. I am curious what a vacation is.

Now the time has come. Our baskets are packed, the food too. Off we went. We drove for a long time. I curled up and slept. We were allowed to romp a lot there and my mistress had a lot of time for us. But the most beautiful was the meeting with my brother. We recognized each other immediately. He is much taller than me and goes to school. This is a place where he learns to behave well. Mistress says I have to go there soon too. It was a wonderful day. Unfortunately, it was over much too quickly and we left again. A few days later we saw each other again. There were many people looking at us. They loo-

Ares

Apollo

Afternoon nap

ked us in the mouth, in the ears and were quite pleased.
They said that we will become something. What do you
think? Well, we will see. My brother has already won a
few awards. My mistress says I still have time until I go to
shows. I am curious. Soon our vacation was over and we
drove home.

I have a lot of fun with my family. There is always some-one who plays with me. Mom cleans me and I am allowed to do everything when she is there. My mistress always says I'm a charmer and you can't refuse me anything.

When I've done something wrong or want something, I put on my saddest dachshund look and hang my ears. That always works. Only once it didn't. I ate my mistress's new shoes. She was angry. No dachshund look helped. She scolded me and I didn't get a good night cookie like the others. I never went to her shoes again. But I can have a lot of fun with my master's socks. I drag them away and hide them. Master runs after me. Mistress says it's his own fault if he always teases me with the socks. Sometimes I pick the socks off the clotheshorse and run back and forth until someone notices and runs after me. It's a great game.

When I'm tired, I snuggle up to my mommy, take one of her ears in my mouth and suck myself to sleep. My mistress always takes it out of my muzzle and scolds me. When she looks away, I just take it back into my mouth and continue sucking carefully.

I have all the freedom with my big buddy Rumpel. I can even steal food from his bowl. Aunt Flo is bitchier. She always grumbles at me. However, she always waits to eat until I sit next to her and keep her company.

Since recently I have a new girlfriend. Her name is Josy and, like Rumpel, she is a rough-haired dachshund. But she is a girl. She is taller than me and her fur is bristly. She is wonderful to play with. We play very well together. Our favorite game is tug-of-war with, guess what, Master's socks, of course. That's fun, making knee socks out of regular socks.

Josy

I love to lie in the sun and doze with my mom. Outside I run around like the wind and if it smells good somewhere, I roll in it. My mistress is not happy about that. She grabs me and then I have to take a bath. Yuck, water! I don't know what Aunt Luna thinks about it. She loves it. She jumps into every pond and collects everything that mistress throws in. Rumpel blows bubbles and kicks like crazy. Mom and I stay on the shore and watch. On Sundays, we all have little pieces of cooked egg. So delicious. When my mistress eats yogurt, we are allowed to lick out the cup. Each of us wants to be the first. Yogurt residue sticks to our noses and the big cleaning begins.

Sometimes our mistress brings strange-smelling animals home. Aunt Luna is totally freaking out. My mistress was then on the hunt. We can all smell it and bite into it. Phew, this fur in the mouth. Well, I don't think it's that great yet. Mistress says, it will be and we will practice it. Soon I will, like my brother, go to a school. This will certainly be interesting. I will tell you about it another time.

Until then your Apollo.

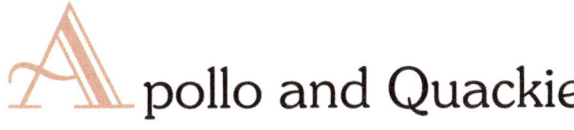 pollo and Quackie

A duckling moves in with us

Hello my dears, I have already told you that my mistress sometimes brings funny smelling animals. Only this time we were not allowed to play with it, it moved, had little feathers and beeped quietly. It got a cage and was allowed to be in the living room. It was a small duckling, the little one had lost touch with her family and had been brought to the practice where my mistress worked. Since my mistress can not say no, she took it home with her. Quackie was the little one's name.

She grew quite fast and soon she got a little house in the garden, with her own pool, so she could learn to swim. I was still a little dachshund male and when I wanted to see who was splashing around in the garden, this duck animal came running towards me flapping its wings wildly, I was scared, my mistress said I ran away screaming wildly, I can't imagine that at all, but when my mistress says that … my mistress never lies. The rest of the summer I avoided this paddling pool. Quackie quickly learned what it means to be a big duck.

In her pool, she learned how to dig, when the grass was wet, she hopped up and down with both feet to flush out small creatures, then bubbled around in the puddle with her little beak, sifting out her food.

Quackie learning to swim . . .

. . . and dig

Slowly she became too big and mistress said, it's time that our Quackie duck is released back into the wild. So one day she packed up food, took Quackie and drove with her to a brook, probably to the brook where she had once hatched from her egg. Here mistress stroked

Quackie's head once again, gave her some food and put her into the brook. Then she walked along the brook and Quackie swam along. Then our mistress hid and watched what Quackie was doing. At first she called for mistress for quite a while and swam in circles a bit excited. Slowly she

got used to the new environment and started to explore it. Suddenly other ducks appeared and Quackie looked interested at her feather friends.

Mistress then slowly walked away from the brook and watched from a distance what was happening. Quackie had a connection and mistress was able to come home to us reassured, although wistfully. She was a bit sad, but my mistress said, Quackie is an animal from nature and there she belongs, otherwise she would not be happy. And of course we don't want to have an unhappy Quackie. We often went to the brook and watched the ducks, surely our Quackie was there and is now happy in the circle of her feather friends.

pollo's great journey

The move

Summer went by and the days became shorter again, the nights colder and the dear sun often hid behind rain clouds. Something was up at our house. So many things disappeared, everywhere were suddenly large boxes, which one could push wonderfully through the area. In these boxes disappeared all our toys, blankets, our beautiful sofa was also suddenly gone. Slowly it seemed strange to me.

Just good that my mom, Aunt Luna, Aunt Flo and Uncle Rumple were not packed. They were all there and so everything was fine. I could cuddle and my mommy cleaned me and took care of me. Mistress said, soon everything will be different, because we are moving. Then it was time, all our baskets were suddenly gone, many cars stood in front of our door and now we were packed. Imagine that, our travel boxes were comfortably laid out with blankets, then we were allowed to snuggle in there and off we went into the car. I knew that, it was like going on vacation. Hm, maybe we were going on vacation?

After a while mistress also got into the car, she said now let's go. Then we were on the road for many hours. In between I got a little cranky, I had to go to the bathroom, I was hungry and wanted to play a little. Mistress always took breaks with us, but we were not allowed to play. Then finally we were there. Here were all our things, our

Apollo (l.) and Aunt Luna (r.) in Ubstadt

Apollo –
cuddling with mom

Luna

Zofe

on the sofa sunbathing

sofa, our baskets and blankets and our food boxes. If I only knew where we are now.

Mistress said we moved from the north to the south. Here the summers are hot and the winters mild, mistress said. Actually not so bad, but we no longer had a garden, I did not like that at all. Mistress said, you will get used to it, well I don't know. It was nice that I should see my little brother very often now. We were now very close to him and because his mistress was not doing so well, he moved back in with us. Wonderful, we played so much,

Apollo, Ares and Rumpel

Rumpel   Luna

teased Uncle Rumpel and slept together curled up with our mom.

After a while everything was cleared, everything had its place and we had settled in. Mistress now worked directly under our apartment. She had much more time for us. Slowly spring arrived. It became warmer, the dear sun was shining more and more often and we were basking in its rays.

One day my mistress told me that now the seriousness of life would begin for me. I was already one year old, a handsome dachshund male. My mistress said that school would soon begin for me. I was already so excited about what that might be – school.

pollo grows up

– the school

On a beautiful April Wednesday afternoon, mistress packed a backpack, a bowl, a blanket and lots of treats. Today was my first day of school. Arrived in the forest, there were many other dogs, lots of dachshunds, they all looked like my uncle Rumpel and other fur-nose buddies too. That was quite exciting.

A funny looking biped told us where to go. He had a beard, a hat and a penetrating voice. Once I was a bit excited and didn't quite listen, and I think I barked a bit too, when a loud voice boomed across the meadow: Apollo, quiet now! I was so scared, Uncle Jürgen made a quick announcement and I listened. My mistress looked at me and said: you see, be nice and quiet. Whenever Uncle Jürgen was around, I made a special effort.

We learned how to „heel", how to sit, how to lay down, run ahead, wait for mistress without whining, lay down and stay and look for mistress. I did that very quickly. My mistress went away from me and hid, then I had to look for her. Well, without my mistress nothing goes, so I swept like lightning through the forest and have always found her very quickly. Now came the wet part, I should actually go into the water and swim. Well, that was not really my thing. My mistress had an idea. My aunt Luna was a real water rat, so she should teach me the joy of water. When I watched her splashing around in the wa-

Apollo and Mistress
at the water

ter, I thought to myself, that looks exciting. The greatest thing was, she always got a toy to take out. So I jumped over my little dachshund shadow and off I hopped into the cool water, I couldn't get enough. That was achieved. After half a year I was done with school.

Now also an exam followed, mistress was so proud of me, I rushed through the thickest blackberry bushes to find her, I did that just for my mistress.

Now the second part began, my mistress said, now comes the dachshund graduation. You know that my mis-

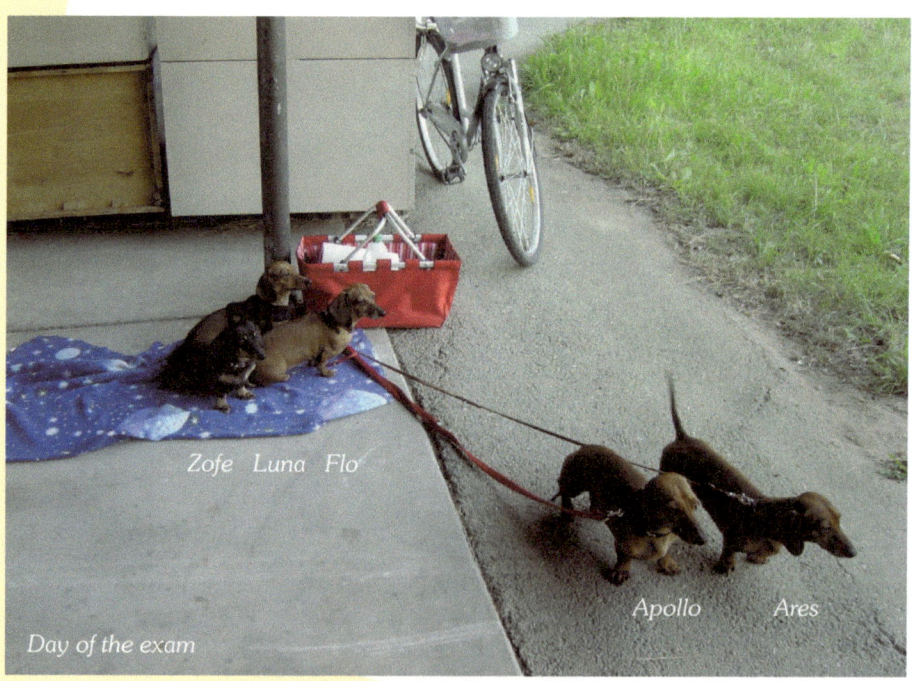

Zofe Luna Flo

Apollo   Ares

Day of the exam

Apollo and Luna in hunting

tress also goes hunting. She said, that is in the dachs-hunds blood. My aunt Luna was a great hunter, of course only together with my mistress. I learned so much from her. She was really passionate, at the age of 8 months she was already out with her mistress looking for deer. She solved her exams with skill and willfulness, always much to the surprise of the examiners.

I searched, became bulletproof and kept my inner peace in every situation. Only one thing I never did again – go through the blackberry bushes, I only did that to look for my mistress. When searching, she always and every time had to carry me around prickly thorny plants, then we went on. My mistress and I also passed this test.

Now a breeding show followed, I was measured, my little teeth were examined and I had to run in a circle, so that they could judge my back line, my little belly and my dachshund legs. My little brother was in the ring with me, so we two brothers ran together. Then that was done. Now I was an adult.

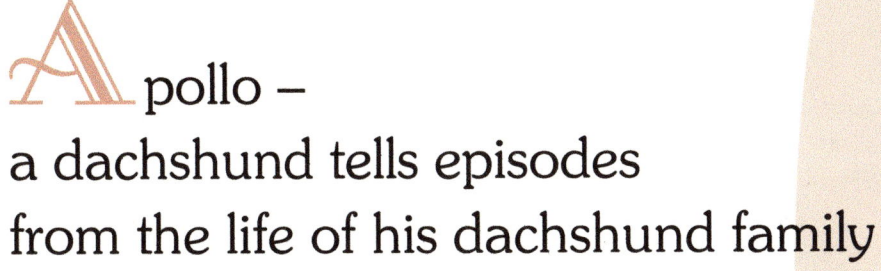

Apollo –
a dachshund tells episodes
from the life of his dachshund family

My sister is born

So slowly we have settled into our new surroundings. We explored the woods and fields and enjoyed our dachshund life to the fullest. One day, when I wanted to romp wildly with my mom, my mistress said: „no Apollo, not today, not so wild, you get little brothers and sisters". Well, I already have a brother and he is not so small anymore, he is even bigger than me. Hm, then I went out and looked for them, no sibling in sight. My mistress laughed and said, I have to be patient a little longer. My mom became more and more round and she didn't want to play with me anymore. But cuddling and cleaning and sucking ears to fall asleep, that was still possible.

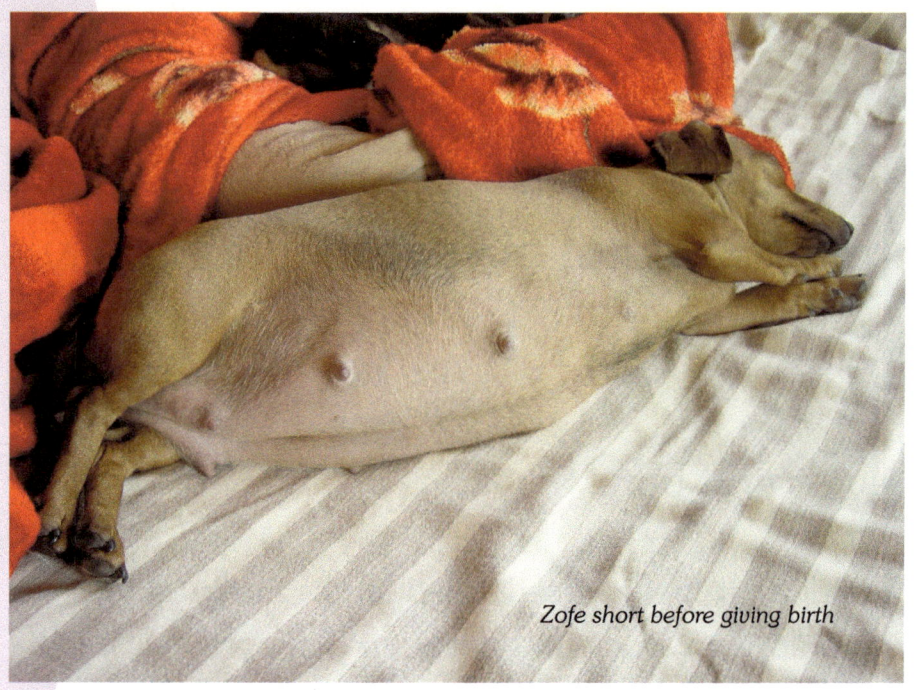
Zofe short before giving birth

After a while, my mistress built a strange thing, four high walls with a door that was locked. In it she put our big car box. It was nicely padded. I sat in front of it and wondered.

One beautiful February morning, the sun was already shining through the windows and little dust flakes were dancing through the air, our mistress suddenly became very hectic. She tells us to be good and not to do anything wrong, then she disappeared with my mom.

After quite a while, I had just been following the sun's rays on the sofa, I heard my mistress's car. She came in with a basket. Therein lay my mom, she looked very sleepy, and 2 little tiny dachshunds. A black and red girl and a red boy. My mistress said to me, they are your brother and sister. My mistress told us that my little brother had grown a little too big and that's why my mommy had to have an operation. But everything went well and now they were here: Bendis aus der Götterdämmerung and Bacchus aus der Götterdämmerung.

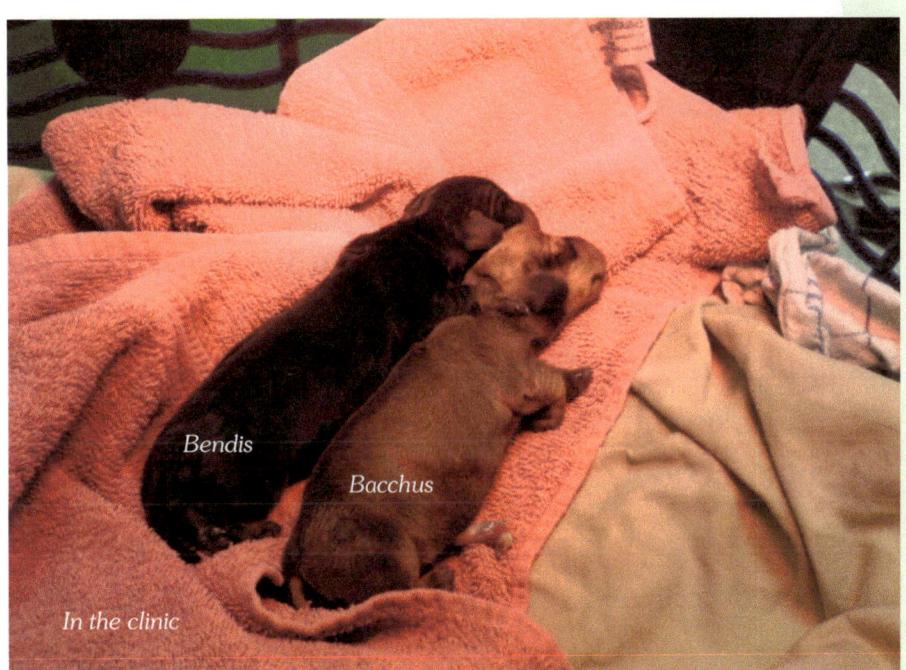

Bendis

Bacchus

In the clinic

Zofe with Bendis and Bacchus

Well, I thought, they are small, how can you play with them? My mistress put my mom and the two little ones in the box. My aunt Luna was very excited, she really wanted to see the little ones. My mom was not so enthusiastic, she grumbled a bit. My mistress said we could go later, but not now.

I missed my mom a bit, she was only with the two little ones, I was not allowed to cuddle with her at all. After a few weeks it got better, Aunt Luna had won her place

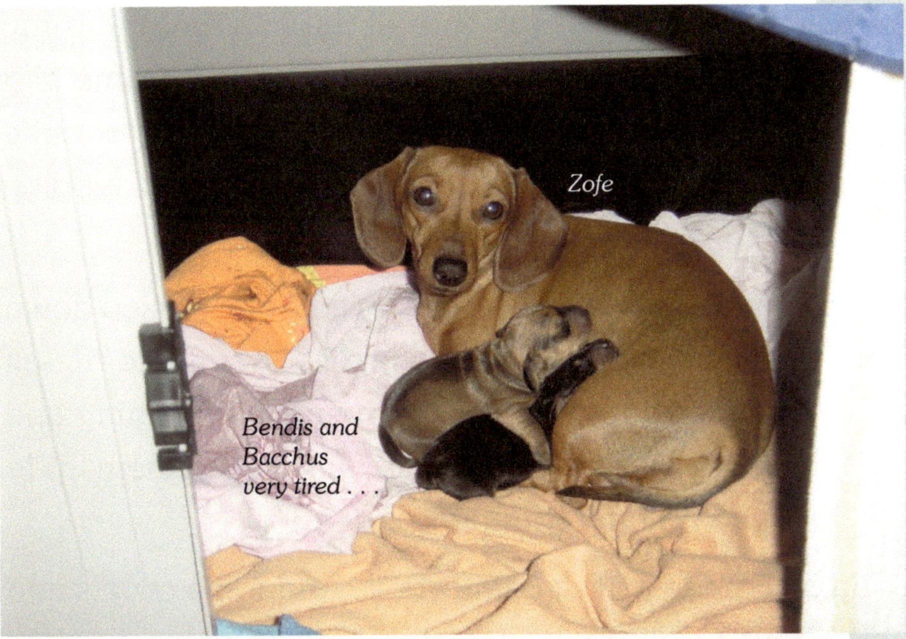

Zofe

Bendis and
Bacchus
very tired . . .

. . . at the milk-bar

in the whelping box, took care of the little ones and my mom had time for me again. When the two became bigger, we were allowed to play together, which was quite exhausting. They were constantly pinching and nipping and teasing.

Uncle Rumpel made sure he got on the sofa, looked down from above and got to safety. Clever, I thought to myself and went after him. The two of them were whining and complaining. Then my mistress came and put them up to us. So again nothing with peace.

I had just made myself comfortable under the covers and was about to disappear into the land of dreams, when suddenly it pinched quite violently on my buttocks. My little brother had actually pinched me in the butt. My mistress just laughed and freed me from the troublemaker. Time flew by. Again and again a two-legged friend came to play with us and the little ones. My mistress said, this will be the new mistress of your little brother. Bacchus, who was now called Waldi, loved his new mistress very much. Whenever she came, she played with him, went out with him and brought treats and toys. One day our mistress said it was now time to say goodbye. Waldi would now have to go to his new home. The nice lady came to us, played with all of us again, Waldi again immediately sat on her lap and licked her. My mistress took him in her arms again and told him to be decent and always listen, we would come to visit him soon. Then she cried a little. My mom looked and searched a bit, but the rest of us comforted her. My little sister Bendis should stay with us. We were one heart and soul, she learned everything from me. When she was supposed to go to school, she was a bit skeptical at first. She was alone, without me. Mistress says she has always looked if I am not somewhere and help her. But then she passed her test with flying colors, even without me. She even went into the water all

by herself. My mistress then went with her to a breeding show and then she was grown up.

Unfortunately, we never saw our little brother again. We lost him in a tragic accident when he was only four months old. Our mistress was terribly sad and his mistress was also inconsolable. The short time he was with us and with his new mistress he gave so much joy and love, we will never forget him.

Bacchus
4 weeks old

Bacchus – 7 weeks old

Another move

The days and weeks went by and quickly became a year. One fine day it became restless again at home. Mistress acted mysteriously. Suddenly boxes and suitcases appeared again, everything was packed and stowed away.

This time the journey didn't take long at all, I had just lounged in the little box when they said we were already there. And then, I could hardly believe my eyes: a garden and a new house.

Apollo in he new home

We got our own room with balcony, from the living room we could go directly to the terrace and garden. Simply wonderful, we could lie in the sun, romp on the lawn and sniff flowers. The neighbors were great, we were petted and had new dog friends.

One winter there was even snow, we swept through the garden like snow bunnies. My Aunt Luna caught snowballs and disappeared with her head in the snow pile, which was fun. It was a nice time.

Luna in the snow

Zofe and Luna – where is the snugglebed

From time to time our mistress had to go on a trip. She always learned something new. Since I was very well-behaved, and always listened well to what my mistress said, I was always allowed to come along. The rest of my family stayed at home and was looked after by the dog sitter or master.

The most educated dachshund

As already mentioned, I was always allowed to come along when my mistress went on trips. I was at seminars, at conferences and congresses. Once I lay on my back for 6 hours and let myself be cuddled. At the same time my belly was examined with an ultrasonic device. Many veterinarians had a look at my inner life and learned. One day a package came addressed to me, with a bag of treats, all for me, because I let myself be scanned so nicely. Of course, I shared them with my family.

Once I was on the road as a model, since I was now very fond of water, I presented an underwater treadmill. At a trade fair in Baden-Baden, I walked quite bravely in the water. So everyone could see how the device works.

From time to time we just sat there and listened, which was sometimes quite tiring. So dark and warm, quiet murmuring and my mistress's lap, my eyes would fall shut from time to time. Once I fell asleep deeply and my mistress said I snored. Quite peacefully and comfortably, the speaker stopped talking and it was quiet as a mouse for a minute. In this minute I started to snore really loud. The whole room heard it and smiled.

I was also with in the most different hotels. My mistress always took my basket and my blankets along. My bowls and my food. I was also allowed to go to restaurants, where I lay down on my blankets and waited until my mistress had finished eating. Everyone was very enthusiastic about how sweet I am.

At the last advanced training course, I was appointed dachshund professor honores causa. I learned a lot about

Apollo waiting for his mistress

X-rays. There you can see on pictures, how we look from the inside. Very rarely I was not there, mostly when my mistress did not go far, or it was not allowed. Then I sat at the door and waited until my mistress was back, then I looked terribly offended and made my mistress feel guilty. That got me extra treats and petting.

Apollo goes to the ballet

I told you that my mistress always took me with her. Once I was a bit sick and my mistress wanted me under observation, so she took me to her ballet class. Well, I was curious what that might be.

I got my little bed and was allowed to cuddle up there. Then I looked at the whole thing. There were other mistresses, they wore funny clothes and stood at a bar. Then they lifted their legs and arms, all to a beautiful music, I almost fell asleep.

Suddenly there was movement in the whole assembly and everyone jumped around and whirled. It quieted down again, they stood and bowed. Then all the fun was over and we drove home.

Well and because I was such a sweet dachshund male, I was allowed to go again and again. I was petted and praised and I always knew when to be quiet and when it was over. As soon as my mistress bowed after twirling around, it was over and I was also allowed to stand up and was petted. I dozed and snuggled nicely to the sounds of Swan Lake.

My two nieces

I have already told you about our dachshund family. This includes Aunt Luna, Uncle Rumpel, Aunt Flo, my mom Zofe, my sister Bendis and me. When we moved into our new house and settled down comfortably, two little dachshund girls joined us. My little sister Bendis became a mommy herself. Two little girls, a black and red and a tiger dachshund girl, saw the light of day in the early morning hours of a friendly September day in a clinic.

My little sister was quite surprised about what suddenly crawled around and squeaked, she was first a bit unsure what to do with it. But our mistress helped her, then everything was all right. She cleaned them and took care of them, but she was quite cranky and barked in her own

Bendis short before giving birth

way like a seal, because she did not want to stay alone with the two. My mistress then agreed with her, as soon as the little ones were asleep, she was allowed to join us. The little ones were named Ceres and Chloe aus der Götterdämmerung.

As they grew up, my mistress built the same little house in the living room again, as she had done with my sister at

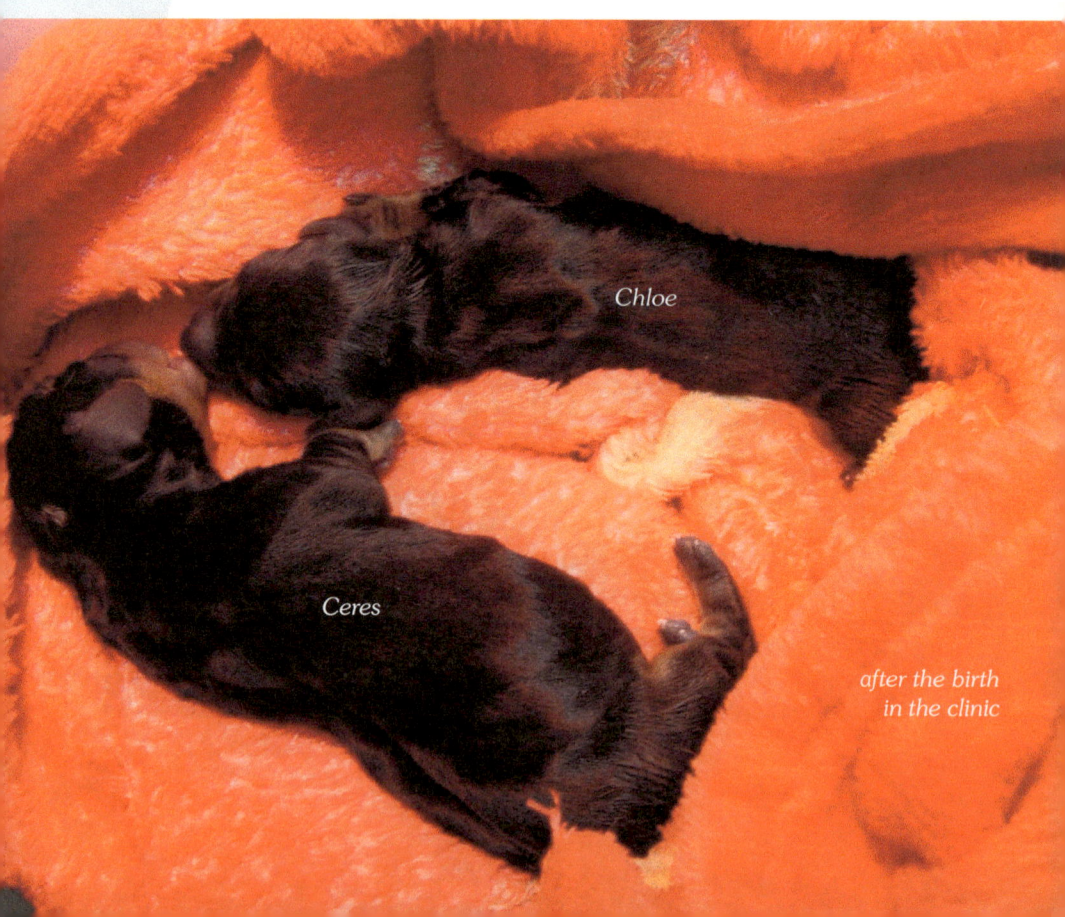

Chloe

Ceres

after the birth in the clinic

Ceres and Chloe – 7 days old

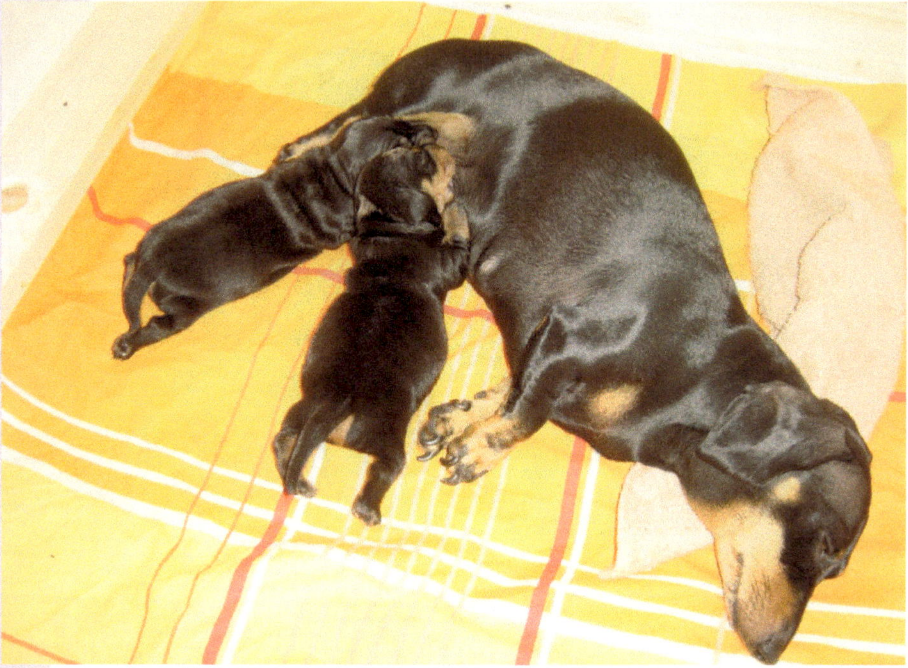

Bendis, Ceres and Chloe in the Whelping Box

that time. Now my sister Bendis was also satisfied, because she could be with us again and the little ones too.

When the two were five weeks old, Chloe suddenly felt very bad. She got bumps all over her body and her ears swelled up. Mistress took her to the university hospital in Giessen. It would take five months for her to recover. My mistress was very unhappy. We were all so happy when she felt better again.

Now there were seven of us. The 7 miniature dachshunds and our mistress.

Apollo goes on vacation

From time to time we packed our baskets, gathered blankets, stowed food and toys. Mistress brought out large bags and packed her things into them. Then we went on vacation. We drove in mistress's car for hiking in the Black Forest, in the snow to St. Engelmar Glashütt, to the coast on the Darß and to Usedom. I could hardly wait until it finally starts, so I already got in the car, but unfortunately my legs are too short, I just can not reach the gas pedal.

Apollo – when does it start

It was wonderful, all day we had mistress only for us and what all have we experienced. In the middle of a snow flurry our vehicle broke down, mistress was not pleased at all, after several attempts we had to leave the vehicle there and all our boxes and crates had to be reloaded into another car.

Sankt Englmar in Snow

When we were at the coast, which is a place with a lot of water and a lot of sand between the paws and many funny looking birds, master drove us around the whole

Flo

island in a bicycle trailer. That was great, we were all allo-wed to snuggle in the back and were chauffeured like that. We were the Bellomobile, everyone who met us laughed.

Darß

Darß

Bendis and Flo

tired after a day at the beach

Ahrenshoop Beach

Apollo at the beach on the Darß

So we have spread a lot of joy. Last year we were also on the road with my mistress and her mom and brother, again to the coast. This time only my aunt Flo and I were with them. My little sister Bendis and my little nieces Ceres and Chloe stayed with their master. My mistress had a little trolley with her, in which Flo and I could sit when we were on the road, or I was allowed to sit in my mistress's backpack. Because my heart is not working so well anymore and I must not overexert myself. It was wonderful, this fresh salty air, this water, first it comes to you, then it runs away from you. I barked at it and it ran away from me and suddenly my feet were wet. We had so much fun.

Apollo – the small Dachshund and the Sea

Apollo and Flo in the Buggy

One day we went to a big city, where my mistress wanted to visit a sea museum, a great house with lots of fish and other sea things, but we two dachshunds were not allowed to come, not even in the buggy. My mistress was not pleased at all. Yes, now she stayed with us in the car, and mistress's mom and brother went alone, then mistress's mom came to us and stayed with us, so mistress could also go to the museum. That's how our mistress is.

Dachshund-Heaven in front of the fireplace in Durbach

We especially like to go to Durbach in the Black Forest. There is a great hotel, very dachshund loving.

We have been there a few times and it's always great, a little fire to warm your dachshund belly and lots of lovely people.

You can walk through the vineyards or, as in my case, be pushed through the beautiful landscape in a trolley. We hiked up to a castle and mistress and master took great pictures.

Durbach

Zofe in front of the vinyards at Castle Staufenberg

Changes –
We are getting older – Aunt Lüni

Changes are also always happening in our lives. No day is like the other, there is always something to discover, experience and we are getting older. In the meantime, a master has moved in with us again.

69

He loves us all very much, plays with us and goes for a walk with us. My aunt Luna, affectionately called Lüni by all of us, became very ill, she could no longer eat on her own. My mistress took her and us everywhere, even to Switzerland, where there were specialists. Lüni got a stomach tube, which was a small tube, through which she got her food. Mistress made it very liquid. She was always very happy, played with us, but she often spit up. She was something very special, everyone knows that he may not mop from the others food bowl. Our Lüni always went very fast to somebody elses bowl, stuffed her cheeks, then went to her bowl, spit it in there and then looked very innocent. If mistress wanted to say something, she couldn't, because it was in her bowl. She was that smart. My little sister Bendis perfected this, she went to Aunt Flo, looked quite unconcerned, stretched out a front paw and pulled the bowl to her in a flash. Then Flo had no more bowl, she had one and from that she ate.

One day mistress said to us that we have to let our Lüni go, she said she was now going to Waldi and to our aunt Vesta, whom we all never met. Vesta was a little dachshund girl who came to mistress when she was a little girl herself. It was her who taught our mistress to love us dachshunds. She was by her side for more than 16 years, then the day came when our mistress had to say goodbye to her. It was a terrible day for our mistress. Our aunt Lüni brought her joy again, she was born in the same kennel as her Vesta 16 years ago. The mommy of our Luna was the sister of my mommy. You see, we were all one big family. My mom Zofe and Aunt Flo were sisters too.

But I digress.

Luna

Mistress cuddled
us all tightly
and took
our Lüni with her.
At home
it became
very quiet
for a while,
we all
missed her
very much.
My mistress
said, now she
is well again
and she watches over all of us.

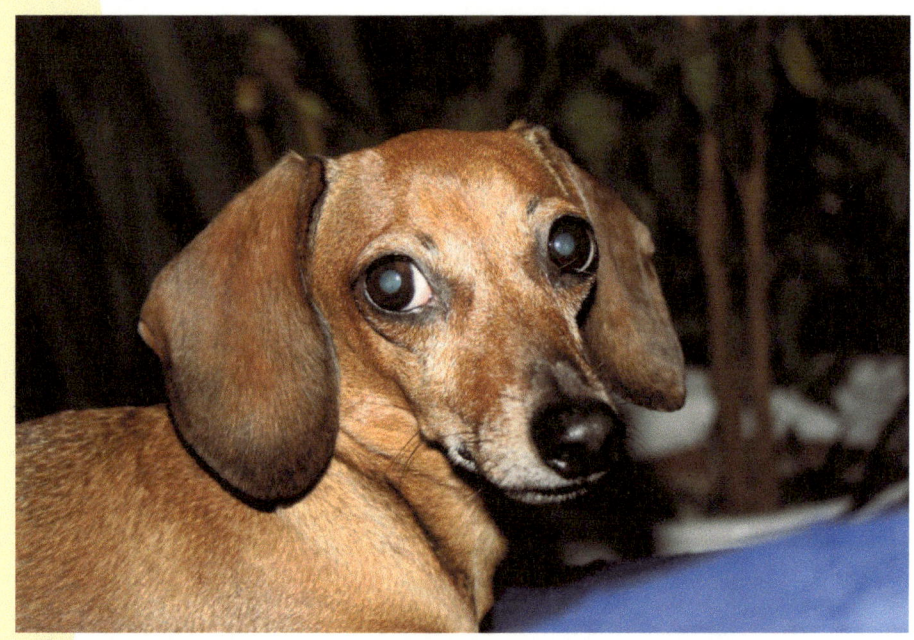

Luna

Our 2 little girls became big girls and Ceres was also allowed to go to school. Chloe was still too fidgety, so she got a grace period and private lessons from a very dear dog trainer. Unfortunately our Chloe got sick again and again and had to be operated, but nothing can get such a brave little girl down. She recovered and was just as much of a whirlwind as before.

Our mistress had meanwhile moved with us to our master, but such a move does not bother me anymore, only for the little ones it was something completely new. For a while we lived in this little house, then it became restless again. Master and mistress were on the road a lot, we spent a lot of time at mistress's practice, I always sat in the registration and watched over everything. I never missed anything.

Our mistress said she would build us a new home, where we would have our own little kingdom, a beautiful garden and a terrace where we could sunbathe as long as we wanted. Then it was – with detours, we have first lived with mistresses mom, because our house was not yet finished – so far, we could move in.

Our new home

For over 2 years now we live in our beautiful domicile, mistress has made everything dachshund-proof, we even have a ramp to walk into the garden. We share the garden with 5 turtles-ladies: Gertrud, Kunigunde, Brunhilde, Emma and Elsa. They have a nice spout with their own small stream and greenhouse to sleep in.

In a small pond lives a family of goldfish and in the tit house lives a family of titmice. My mistress has a greenhouse in which many delicious plants grow. She has planted strawberries, blackberries and raspberries, and we are allowed to pick a ripe berry at any time. Our Chloe can do this very well, she tips her lips and plucks the berries very carefully from the stalks. I wait until my mistress does that and brings me the treat.

We all feel very comfortable here, mistress has her practice under our cottage and therefore has much more time for us. Unfortunately we had to let go my beloved Mama Zofe to our aunt Lüni last year. She fell asleep peacefully in the arms of mistress, we were all around her, so she

Kunigunde

Brunhilde, Kunigunde, Gertrud

Family Goldfisch

Flo

Ceres

Apollo

Zofe

sunbathing

Chloe and Apollo

Ceres
Zofe
Apollo

Mom Zofe

was not alone. I miss her very much. She was my haven of peace, and always treated me like her little puppy, even though I was all grown up. Chloe took her place in mistress' bed. She looked for her place very carefully piece by piece. My aunt Flo is already a gray eminence. She is the old lady of our family. She sleeps a lot now, but as soon as one of us wants to have his ears cleaned, she is wide awake and cleans us. She cleans and licks us

Mom Zofe

Aunt Flo

with a devotion of her own. Mistress says we have to en-joy every day while our Flöhchen is still with us. She has developed a funny peculiarity, she takes a piece of food from her bowl, brings it into the dining room, puts it on the carpet, looks around, then gets another piece, which she then eats and so it goes on and on until the bowl is empty. In between she goes to drink, then into the garden and then eats again, a real ritual.

In the meantime we have become a small dachshund community, Flöhchen is indeed the grey eminence, but after Aunt Lüni had crossed the rainbow bridge, I took over and led the pack. My mom and mistress helped me. I have led and mediated disputes, a beautiful, but sometimes difficult task. When my mistress noticed that it became too much for me, she took me and gave me a vacation time. Ceres is sometimes especially pushy, she always wants to please me and is constantly cleaning my mouth. My little sister Bendis is already 11 years old, my little nieces 8 years and yes, I am now also 13 years old.

An older dachshund gentleman, still a little dachshund man in his head, remembering all the good and sad times.

Chloe   Bendis   Ceres

Apollo

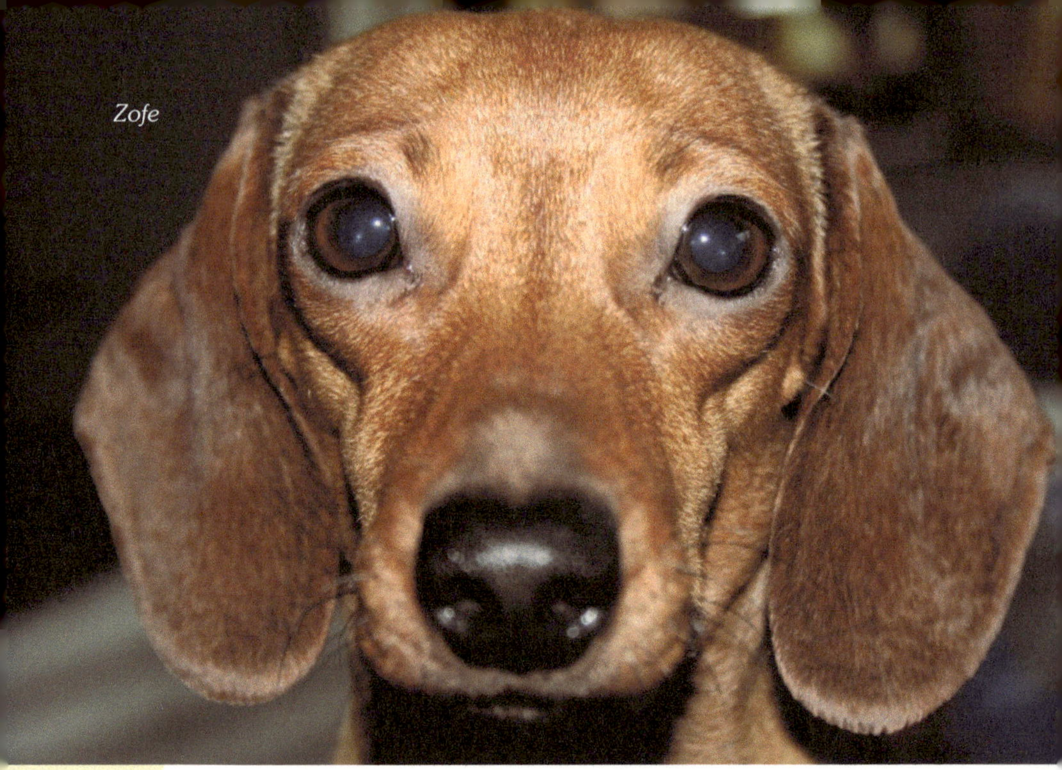

Zofe

Ceres   Bendis   Apollo   Chloe

My task as a scribbler

I have been given the task of writing down everything my little family has experienced, but that's not all. Even now I support mistress by always writing down small anecdotes, news and interesting facts for their practice. I even have a small fan base. Sometimes I just chat a little bit out of the sewing box.

When I'm not feeling so well, because my little heart is very sick and a little cancer animal is fighting in my body, my little sister Bendis takes my place. She is always very upset, but I calm her down and say, „You'll do it. Well, and then it works.

WE ARE FAMILY 🐾

Chloe   Apollo   Flo   Zofe   Ceres   Bendis

So my dears, this was or is my story, I hope you enjoyed it.

All the best to all of you, stay fond of us dachshunds, we are a headstrong, always eager to learn, inquisitive, deeply loyal people who go through fire for our masters and mistresses. My mistress always says that without us the world would only be half as beautiful, well and what would half a world be.

Your Apollo aus der Götterdämmerung

Frauchen und ich

Anne Teutschbein-Licha grew up in Berlin and, at the age of 10, cracked her piggy bank for her first dachshund lady, called Vesta. After studying veterinary medicine, she moved to Niedersachsen. There she worked in a clinic for small animals and a practice for large animals and founded the kennel „aus der Götterdämmerung". Apollo was born here. After moving to Baden-Württemberg, she opened her own practice for small animals in Ubstadt in 2009. After Apollo was enjoying a growing fan base on Facebook, she decided to let him write his own book.

Apollo's epilogue

You know that a dachshund must always have the last word. Sometimes it is also a quite sad one. After this little booklet was finished, we unfortunately had to say good-bye to my aunt Flo. Our Flo was born with the sonorous name „Xandria von der schönen Weide". She was the smallest puppy that saw the light of day in this kennel. That's why she got the nickname „Flo". A small miniature dachshund girl became an even smaller rabbit dachshund girl. On a show this was even officially stated. Yes, our Flo moved from the miniature dachshund studbook to the rabbit dachshund studbook.

Unfortunately, we cannot stop time and the years go by. As an elderly lady she still cleaned us and checked the ears. No one left the house unwashed. Mistress says she is now with my mom and with aunt Lüni and Vesta. She just went ahead, she will always be with us, we will miss her very much.

Your Apollo